MAMA'S DAY

To my mother, Joyce Ashman, with much love—L. A.

To Dusan—J. O.

SIMON & SCHUSTER BOOKS FOR YOUNG READERS
An imprint of Simon & Schuster Children's Publishing Division
1230 Avenue of the Americas, New York, New York 10020
Text copyright © 2006 by Linda Ashman
Illustrations copyright © 2006 by Jan Ormerod
SIMON & SCHUSTER BOOKS FOR YOUNG READERS is a trademark of Simon & Schuster, Inc.
Book design by Daniel Roode
The text for this book is set in Venetian.
The illustrations are rendered in pencil and wash.
Manufactured in China
2 4 6 8 10 9 7 5 3 1
Library of Congress Cataloging-in-Publication Data
Ashman, Linda.
Mama's day / by Linda Ashman ; illustrated by Jan Ormerod—1st ed.
p. cm.
Summary: In rhyming text, mothers and their babies are described sharing in a variety of activities,
from playing at the ocean to reading books and taking a bath.
ISBN-13: 978-0-689-83475-2
ISBN-10: 0-689-83475-6
[1. Mother and child—Fiction. 2. Stories in rhyme.] I. Ormerod, Jan, ill. II. Title.
PZ8.3.A775 Mam 2002
[E]—dc21 00-045063

Linda Ashman   Jan Ormerod
MAMA'S DAY

Simon & Schuster Books for Young Readers
New York   London   Toronto   Sydney

Linda Ashman   Jan Ormerod
MAMA'S DAY

Simon & Schuster Books for Young Readers

New York   London   Toronto   Sydney

Somewhere there's a mama lifting baby from a crib,

Snapping rompers, looping laces,
Brushing crumbs from baby's bib.

Somewhere there's a mama holding baby in her lap,

Playing games and making music,
Teaching baby how to clap.

There's a mama by the ocean, holding tight to baby's hand,

Chasing waves and watching seagulls,
Finding seashells in the sand.

Somewhere there's a mama on a busy city street,
Buying flowers, greeting neighbors,
Guiding baby's little feet.

There's a mama in the garden,
Sharing secrets and a snack.

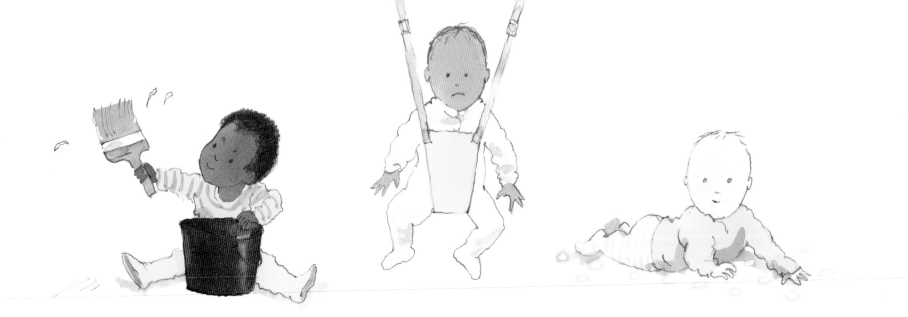

There's a mama in the market with a baby on her back.

Somewhere there's a mama bathing baby's tiny toes,
Splashing water, blowing bubbles,
Wiping suds from baby's nose.

There's a mama rocking baby in a creaky wooden chair,
Reading books and telling stories,
Kissing baby's silky hair.

Somewhere there's a mama soothing baby's tired cries,
Swaying slowly, hushing softly,
Singing quiet lullabies.

There are mamas near and distant

doing just what mamas do:

Loving babies every minute,

every day . . .

like I love you.